10 9 8 7 6 5 4 3 2 1

Library of Congress Cataloging in Publication Data
Robb, Brian.
My grandmother's djinn.
SUMMARY: The entire family helps grandmother's djinn search for his wife whom he hasn't seen in 1000 years.
[1. Fantasy] I. Title.
PZ7.R5317My 1976b [E] 77-22646
ISBN 0-8193-0917-6 ISBN 0-8193-0918-4 lib. bdg.

MY GRANDMOTHER'S DJINN

By BRIAN ROBB

PARENTS' MAGAZINE PRESS
NEW YORK

Published by Parents' Magazine Press 1978
First published by Andre Deutsch Limited, London

Printed in the United States of America

When I was a boy, my grandmother's medicine cabinet held row upon row of bottles with long names on their labels. But the third bottle from the right on the top shelf was special. Its label just said—THE DJINN.

Now djinns have magical powers. Like fine wines, they keep for years in bottles. This bottle had been there as long as my grandmother could remember. Her mother had told her that the djinn has been shut inside for hundreds of years. Nobody had ever dared to open it for fear of what might happen, since once the djinn got out it might be hard to get him back.

But my sister Ursula was by nature adventurous, and on her eighth birthday she borrowed a corkscrew from the kitchen and let the djinn out. I happened to be passing by at the time and heard the pop of the cork, followed by a loud bang, a smell of sulphur, and the appearance of a strange figure that trailed off into vapor where the rest of us have legs.

He had a turban, a little white beard and a very kind face. So Ursula thought it safe to treat him as a friend. But she made him promise to get back into his bottle whenever he heard grownups around.

He kept his word, too, until a sudden scream from the cleaning woman, some six weeks later, made it clear that he had moved too slowly to escape her notice.

My grandmother took the news calmly. She let us keep the cork loose in the djinn's bottle and the cupboard door unlocked so that he could come and go as he pleased. He was useful in many ways. For instance, when she forgot to buy something at the grocery store, he would produce it by magic for free. He was also a first-rate handyman.

But the djinn really won her heart the day that the chimney got blocked. He went up it boldly and came out at the top, black with soot but triumphantly brandishing the bird's nest that had caused the trouble.

His appearance on that occasion created quite a stir in the neighborhood. So my grandmother decided in future to keep him indoors and hide his presence from friends and neighbors. This meant swearing the cleaning woman to secrecy and confining the djinn to his bottle whenever we had guests.

After so many years in solitude, the djinn thoroughly enjoyed our company. He could tell fortunes and knew an endless number of Arabian Nights stories. We would have been only too proud to show him off to our friends, and the djinn would have loved it.

My grandmother's decision came as a blow to him, but he bore her no grudge.

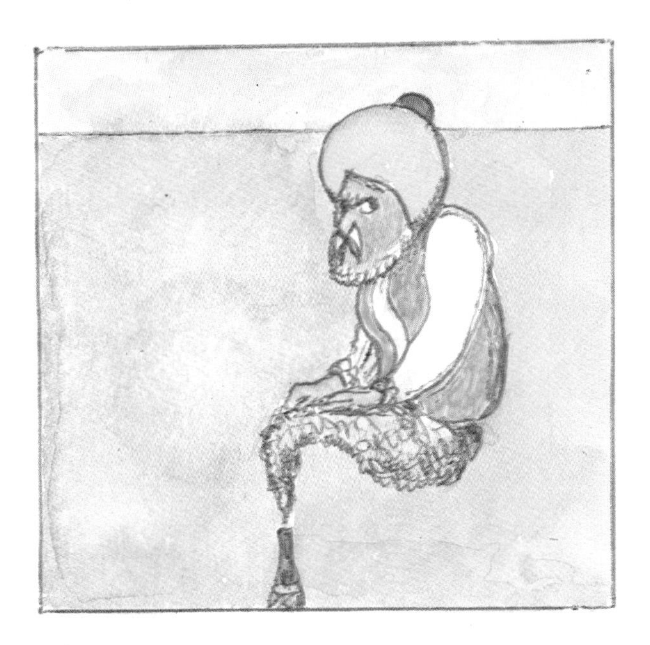

The only outward sign of his feelings was a certain sad expression when he reluctantly retreated into his little glass prison.

Meanwhile Ursula tried to make life less dreary for him by moving his bottle around the house, and making sure the cork was loose enough to let him push his way out whenever he felt desperate. Every time he did so, the pops and bangs he emitted made us jump almost out of our skins.

He was gentle, and we soon grew fond of him. My sister Ursula was his protector, but my Uncle Bertrand and his cat, Gertrude, became the djinn's next best friends.

Uncle Bertrand used to drive down from Yorkshire once or twice a year, bringing Aunt Phyllis and their cat Gertrude in their five-seater touring car. Having served in the East, Uncle Bertrand could speak to the djinn in his native Arabic. The two soon became fast friends, and talked late into the night of cities like Samarkand and Baghdad, or of the open desert where the djinn had passed his childhood. Gertrude generally listened from the top of the kitchen heater.

At first these chats cheered the djinn up quite a lot, but he soon lapsed into melancholy. And one day, when we came home from a walk, Ursula found him perched on top of the kitchen cabinet in a flood of tears.

"I'm sorry to be such a nuisance," he sobbed, "but I'm not quite myself. It isn't that I don't like living in your delightful family with your respected grandmother (sob), your thoughtful brother (sob), your kind uncle, his interesting wife and their understanding cat, not to mention your gracious self (sob). My grief lies in the fact that your happy family has awakened painful memories of the life I once enjoyed long ago in the East with my own dear wife (sob), until the day when it was decreed that all djinns should be confined in bottles. In the confusion, my wife and I somehow got put into separate ones (sob).

"Since that accursed day we have never seen one another, and you have no idea how I miss her."

After a sob or two more, he withdrew and curled up as tight as a cat in his bottle, which gradually filled with his tears till they threatened to drown him. He had spoken with such feeling that Ursula resolved then and there to help him find his wife.

She waited patiently beside his bottle, calling softly to him. Eventually she succeeded in coaxing him out. She gently suggested that his wife might still be alive and well, just as he was. And that it might be possible to find her.

At first the djinn was pessimistic. It had been so long since he had seen her. But Ursula was an optimist. After cross-examining him on the details of exactly where and when it had all happened, she managed to kindle a slender hope. And this, after discussions with my Uncle Bertrand, much thought and much study of maps, gradually ripened into a plan for a rescue operation.

The very idea brought the djinn new joy. He was forever springing out of his bottle with suggestions for the equipment we would need. He even persuaded my grandmother to let him go shopping with us, carefully hidden in his bottle in a wicker hamper. With his help we gradually collected everything necessary for such an adventure—

tents, guns, safari hats, campstoves, sand tracks, mosquito nets, cans of corned beef, bottled water, desert boots, sun lotion, and kerosene lamps, to mention just a few.

One morning when the djinn and I were alone in the house, I answered the door to a peddler buying old junk. He had a long black mustache and seemed only too eager to buy anything—even the djinn's bottle which stood on the hall table. He went so far as to offer ten dollars for it and grew quite angry when I refused him. Luckily I had kept the door on the chain and had no trouble shutting it in his face. I could hear the djinn bubbling over with indignation at the fellow's nerve. He was clearly upset and I was glad I had dealt so firmly with the rogue.

We planned our expedition for the autumn in order to avoid the heat of an African summer. Late in September, Ursula, the djinn, Uncle Bertrand, Gertrude, and I sailed for North Africa. The sky was blue and the sun shone over a sea as smooth as a millpond. So we let the djinn out of his hamper to enjoy the fine weather. To our surprise, he seized a rug we had brought along and flew on it over our heads for the rest of the way, taking Gertrude with him.

A magic carpet was a rare sight. In those days, an airplane was hardly less so. But just as we neared Algiers, a small biplane flew over and buzzed us, its French pilot even leaning out and jeering at the djinn's old-style aircraft. The djinn seemed to understand his French only too well, and the force of his reaction astonished us all. Swelling in size until I thought he would burst, he shouted terrible insults in Arabic. Then, trailing vapor like a modern jet, he chased that biplane out of sight. This side of his character made a deep impression on us.

Once we reached North Africa everthing changed. The djinn was on home territory and showed unexpected powers of leadership. Even after all these years, I still have a vivid picture of our little caravan heading into the desert from the small town of El Hadj. My Uncle Bertrand, with Ursula at his side, drove the five-seated car laden with camping equipment, and I followed on a camel. The djinn, now in his element, sailed overhead on his magic carpet with Gertrude beside him.

We passed through Arab villages with mosques, cactuses and palms, where we traded tea for local produce such as dates, eggs and some rather odd-tasting wine. The crossing of the desert was monotonous, hot, and harder work than we had expected, because the car kept sinking into soft sand and had to be dug out. But we also had time to relax, and the djinn soon became a good cricket player.

I shall never forget his joy when we got our first distant glimpse of the mountains we had to climb to reach Buj, the city where he had been put in his bottle—and the place where we now hoped to find his wife.

Just before dusk, we stopped for the night at a village in the foothills. Having pitched our camp, Ursula and I went for a walk to stretch our legs.

The village street was dark and deserted. Lighted windows were rare. The sound of oriental music and the sight of shadowy figures in doorways were the only signs of habitation. So we were surprised to see a little red car draw up outside what looked like the village inn. The man who got out wore a fez, but otherwise western-style clothes. He had a long black mustache which, in the half-light, struck me as being vaguely familiar.

Next day, we started so early that we reached Buj and found rooms in a hotel before noon. The journey had been uneventful. The only other traveler we had seen on the road had been the black-mustached man in the fez, who passed us in his little red car, staring in amazement at the djinn flying overhead.

We decided to begin our search in the café attached to the hotel. There was just one other customer sitting alone at a corner table.

The waiter, while clearly aware that Buj had once been famous for its djinns, assured us that there had never been any at all in his day. So we sat down at a bamboo table and gloomily sipped iced coffee, to the tune of heartbroken sobs from the wicker hamper. After so much planning and traveling, the disappointment was almost unbearable. Even Ursula seemed in despair.

It was then, as I recall, that the only other customer stood up, sidled rather like a crab towards us and bowed. He declared, in hesitant English, that he could perhaps be of assistance. Had he correctly overheard that we were interested in djinns? If so, a friend of his had, in fact, built up a unique collection. Some even said that it included every djinn surviving in the world, apart from a single specimen reputed to exist in England. All of them were, moreover, alive and in their original bottles, which of course added greatly to their value.

This raised our hopes. If it were true, our djinn's wife might well be among the number! So after a brief consultation with Uncle Bertrand, it was agreed that this crablike person should return after siesta and take us to see his friend.

We were in an agony of suspense until about five o'clock, when he came and led us to a fine house a few streets away. I was astonished to see parked outside it that same little red car! And the man who opened the door for us wore a fez and had a very long black mustache.

It was, in fact, the same face. But it was too dead-pan to show the least sign of recognizing us. And the question ceased to be of interest when he

opened yet another door leading into a huge room full of row upon row of bottled djinns neatly stacked on shelves.

Uncle Bertrand stayed in the hallway explaining to the black-mustached man and his crablike friend just what we wanted. Ursula, Gertrude the cat, and I meanwhile walked into the room lined with bottles, carrying my grandmother's djinn in his hamper.

And then I suddenly remembered whose face the black-mustached man's reminded me of. It was the peddler who had come to our house in England and shown such an interest in our own djinn's bottle!

When I told Ursula, she saw at once that we were intended victims of a cunning plot, aimed simply at acquiring our djinn to complete the black-mustached man's collection. To prevent this, we had to make our own plan, and we decided the captive djinns might prove useful allies in case of emergency. So we went about loosening as many corks as possible in their bottles on the shelves.

By sheer luck we loosened the last cork at the very moment my uncle finished his negotiations. It seems he had agreed that we would call again the next morning to hear whether the black-mustached man was willing to sell us my grandmother's djinn's wife—if he had her. And if so, for how much.

We arrived at about eleven and were again received in the hall, where for a few moments the black-mustached man kept up a pretense of making a deal. Then, without warning, he seized our djinn's wicker hamper, dashed with it into the room where he kept his own djinns, and locked the door. Our suspicions had been correct.

A clever plan. But he had not counted on the fact that my grandmother's djinn had a loosely corked bottle and a very fierce temper. Peeking through the keyhole, we saw him burst out of both bottle and hamper, swelling with rage as he did so to a quite exceptional size, and emitting the fieriest of fumes and the loudest conceivable bangs.

"Djinns," he roared, knowing that we had loosened all their corks, "Djinns, arise from your bottles." They needed no second prompting. The popping, banging and roaring that now ensued were deafening even to us in the next room.

And they were followed almost immediately by the collapse of the door under the combined attack of innumerable angry and excited djinns bent on escape.

These creatures now ransacked the house for all the carpets they could find. And, for several days, they could be seen flying away in various directions, never to be heard from again.

At last we entered the room. The black-mustached man lay in a faint, while the room's only other occupants—my grandmother's djinn and his beautiful wife—stood clasped in a fond embrace. Tears of happiness ran down their cheeks.

It was a touching reunion after perhaps a thousand years of separation. And we all solemnly promised that they should never again be parted. So, when we got back to England, Ursula and I bought a bottle big enough to hold them both.

This stood for many years in my grandmother's medicine cabinet, with a label reading THE DJINNS—PLEASE KNOCK. It now stands beside me as I write. Unlike myself, its inhabitants, are quite untouched by time, for djinns, of course, always remain the same.